The Enchanted Snow Pony

For Annette & Nest, my fairy godmothers xx
—*SARAH KILBRIDE*

To Christine
—*SOPHIE TILLEY*

ALADDIN
An imprint of Simon & Schuster Children's Publishing Division
1230 Avenue of the Americas, New York, New York 10020
First Aladdin hardcover edition November 2022
Text copyright © 2015 by Sarah KilBride
Jacket illustration copyright © 2022 by Paula Franco
Interior illustrations based on artwork originated by Sophie Tilley copyright © 2015
Originally published in Great Britain in 2015 by Simon & Schuster UK Ltd.
Also available in an Aladdin paperback edition.
All rights reserved, including the right of reproduction in whole or in part in any form.
ALADDIN and related logo are registered trademarks of Simon & Schuster, Inc.
For information about special discounts for bulk purchases, please contact Simon & Schuster Special Sales at 1-866-506-1949 or business@simonandschuster.com.
The Simon & Schuster Speakers Bureau can bring authors to your live event. For more information or to book an event contact the Simon & Schuster Speakers Bureau at 1-866-248-3049 or visit our website at www.simonspeakers.com.
Jacket designed by Tiara Iandiorio
The text of this book was set in Sabon LT Std.
Manufactured in the United States of America 0922 FFG
2 4 6 8 10 9 7 5 3 1
Library of Congress Control Number 2022936651
ISBN 9781534476370 (hc)
ISBN 9781534476363 (pbk)
ISBN 9781534476387 (ebook)

Princess EVIE

By Sarah KilBride

Interior illustrations by
Sophie Tilley

The Enchanted Snow Pony

ALADDIN
NEW YORK   LONDON   TORONTO   SYDNEY   NEW DELHI

CHAPTER 1

Frozen Fountains

It was a chilly winter's morning at Starlight Castle. Princess Evie was cozy in her nest of duvets with the velvet curtains drawn around her four-poster bed.

As Evie snuggled up, she heard her kitten, Sparkles, push open the bedroom door.

"Good morning, Sparkles," said Evie, peeping out from the thick curtains.

"Meow," he replied cheerfully.

She hopped down from her bed and gave Sparkles his morning hug, then opened the curtains. Evie and Sparkles looked out of the tall windows and saw that Starlight Castle's grounds were white with snow and all the towers and turrets glittered with icicles.

"I think today's going to be a magical day, Sparkles," said Evie. "It's

the winter solstice, which means it's the shortest day of the year. Something special is bound to happen."

Evie and Sparkles didn't waste any time in getting ready. As soon as Evie had finished her breakfast of porridge and berries, they went skipping through the castle grounds to see Evie's magic ponies. They took the shortcut through the fern garden. It had been so cold in the night that even the fountains had frozen, leaving cascades of beautiful icicles.

"Wow, Sparkles!" said Evie. "They look like crystal crowns."

They didn't stop to admire the beautiful icicles for very long. They had to keep moving to stay warm. Besides, Evie could hear all her ponies neighing and getting excited at the thought of breakfast. She smiled from behind her woolly scarf. She loved every one of her ponies—they weren't any old ponies, they were magic ponies.

Whenever Evie rode them through the tunnel of trees, they would take her on the most amazing adventures in faraway lands. Everything changed when they came out of the tunnel— her ponies' coats, their bridles and saddles, manes and tails, and, best of all, Evie's outfits! Once, Evie had been a bridesmaid with a dress the color of bluebells. There she had met Bella and her mischievous pet dragon, Loki. They always made such lovely friends on their adventures—star princesses, ice pixies, and even mermaids.

Evie was brought back down to

earth as a sharp gust of wind blew from the north.

"Brrr, I'm glad I put my thermals on, Sparkles!" she said as she picked up her little kitten and tucked him into her coat. "It's no fun riding in the cold if you haven't wrapped up."

At this time of year, Evie always made sure she wore layers of clothes when she went out riding. She couldn't do without her woolly socks, scarf, and

thermal gloves. Even Sparkles appeared to be wearing an extra layer too—his winter coat was so thick!

"How about warming up with an adventure, Sparkles?" said Evie.

Although Sparkles was only a cat, he must have understood, as he started to purr loudly from under Evie's coat.

Evie unlatched the gate into Starlight Stables and took extra care as she made her way across the yard. There was ice everywhere and it was so slippery that she lost her footing a few times. Feeding in the wintertime always seemed to take longer, but luckily Evie didn't have to groom every pony. Her hardy ponies were happy to stay outside, as the oils in their coats helped to insulate them.

Willow, her New Forest pony,

Indigo, her Haflinger, and Silver, Evie's
dappled Welsh mountain pony, all
whinnied from the gate. Their breath
misted like puffs of smoke.

"Come on, Silver," said Evie. "Let's
go for an adventure."

Evie brought her pony in from the
paddock and tied her next to a net full
of tasty hay. Silver was one of Evie's

smallest ponies—at only twelve hands high. But she was one of the strongest and most determined ponies Evie had ever met. Evie checked her pony over to make sure she was fit, and then

cleaned out her hooves with a hoof-pick. Silver sensed that they were going to ride through the tunnel of trees and began to whicker.

When Princess Evie finished this job, she walked carefully across the icy yard to the tack room, where she found Sparkles curled up on a comfortable old blanket that used to sit under Indigo's saddle.

"Come on." Evie smiled. "I'm going to tack Silver up. She can't wait to take us through the tunnel."

"Meow," replied Sparkles. He loved going on adventures with Evie and her magic ponies and never missed a chance to go through the tunnel of trees with them. They checked through Evie's backpack of useful things and added a few little extras—just in case.

"We've got one more job to do before we leave, Sparkles," said Evie.

She went to the feed room and filled a scoop with a selection of oats, cracked corn, and chopped apples.

"We mustn't forget the birds," said Evie as she sprinkled the contents of the scoop onto the top of the wall in the yard. "This weather can be really tough for our feathered friends."

While Evie had been looking after her ponies, all the wild birds had been searching for scraps to eat. Sparkles watched as Evie gave them fresh water in a shallow dish, and Evie noticed his tail swishing and his long whiskers twitching.

"Sparkles, I hope you're not feeling

hungry after your lovely big breakfast,"
she said.

Luckily it wasn't long before Silver
was tacked up and the little kitten was
perched in the saddle with Evie.

"I wonder who will be waiting for
us," whispered Evie.

They rode away from the stables

and across the fields. Princess Evie
took a deep breath and closed her eyes,
as Silver tossed her thick mane and
trotted into the glittering tunnel of
trees.

CHAPTER 2

Snowflake Surprises

Princess Evie opened her eyes when she heard Silver's hooves crunching through a thick blanket of snow. She was surprised to see it was dark. Not as dark as night; more like dusk. There was no sign of the sun and the sky was heavy with snow clouds.

"I thought it was the morning, Sparkles," said Evie. Her little cat snuggled up to the lovely warm coat that Evie was now wearing. It was made of pale blue felt decorated with snowflakes and the collar was folded up high to protect Evie's face from the cold. Evie wore a pair of white leather gloves to keep her hands warm, and snug winter boots lined with wool.

Silver's mane and tail were decorated with glittering snow crystals and little icicles hung from her reins, tinkling as she shook her head. Evie loosened the reins and Silver lowered her head and neighed loudly, announcing their arrival.

The surrounding snow-filled valley seemed to absorb the sound. There was no echo and no answer. Evie searched the landscape.

"That's strange," said Evie. "Usually, there's somebody waiting for us when we come out of the tunnel."

The three of them looked around,
but there was no one in sight.
Suddenly, this stillness was filled with
a shriek that made Sparkles, Silver,
and Princess Evie jump. They looked
up and saw a raven in the branches of
a bare, black tree. He looked down at
them keenly with shining eyes.

"Hello," said Evie, "were you
expecting us?"

The raven swooped down and landed on the snow in front of them. He looked first at Evie and Sparkles, then at Silver, with his head cocked to one side. Evie thought that he might speak to them, but instead he cawed and began doing a funny little dance, hopping and zigzagging in the snow. He looked around at them with his bright eyes and cawed again.

"I think he wants us to follow him," whispered Evie. He flew up into the air, circled them three times, and then began to fly on ahead. Evie was right—he did want them to follow him.

Silver was sure-footed and sturdy, but had to take her time lifting her hooves high to walk through the deep snow. The raven waited for them on

frozen branches, flying off again when
Silver caught up with him. The promise
of a snowstorm was growing as the
snow clouds grew heavier in the sky.
Evie hoped that wherever they were
going, it wasn't going to be much
farther. Then she realized that they
were walking alongside a frozen lake.

"This looks like Lake Perla," Evie whispered to her pony, "where we went ice-skating with the snow fairies."

Silver whinnied and the raven crowed loudly from above and did a loop in the air.

"I think our raven friend is telling us that this *is* Lake Perla!" said Evie. "Oh, wouldn't it be lovely to see the snow fairies again?"

The three of them had had such fun with Sylvie and Trina, the snow fairies.

"What an adventure!" said Evie with a smile. "Do you remember how we rescued the little polar bear cub that was lost in a snowdrift? I'll never forget how brave you were, Silver. You pulled the snow fairies' sleigh through the blizzard, all the way to the North

Pole, and we delivered the polar bear cub back to his family."

Sparkles purred as he listened to Evie tell the story of their adventure, and Evie knew that talking to Silver was helping to keep her pony's spirits up.

"The polar bears were so grateful that they used their magic powers to help us fly back to the banks of Lake Perla where all the other snow fairies were waiting for us."

Just as Evie mentioned the words *snow fairies*, the snowstorm began and large snowflakes fell from the sky.

If only we could fly through the sky now, Evie thought.

She knew that plodding through thick snow was exhausting for her pony, and now Silver would have to plough on through the blizzard. It

was so cold that when the freezing
snowflakes landed on Evie's eyelashes
they didn't melt. Sparkles tried to catch
the flakes as they fell around him and
Silver's coat glittered with those that
had landed on her.

Evie looked up and saw two huge
flakes swirling and dancing in the
sky. As they swirled, they appeared
to grow. They flew and flurried and

transformed into two shimmering
snow fairies. They were Evie's friends
Sylvie and Trina.

"Hello, Evie," said Sylvie as she
fluttered down, landing gently on the
fresh snow.

The moment Sylvie and Trina landed, the snowstorm stopped.

"Hello, Sparkles and Silver," said Trina, brushing the snow from Silver's coat. "Welcome back."

"I'm so glad you've come to see us," said Sylvie. "When we heard Odin's call we hoped that you had come through the tunnel of trees."

Odin, the raven, flew down and landed on Sylvie's shoulder. Sylvie stroked his glossy feathers.

"It's so lovely to see you again," said Trina. "And today is such a special day. It's the winter solstice and we are going to Queen Aurora's Midwinter Ball."

"Queen Aurora is the snow queen, the queen of the northern skies," explained Trina.

"Will you come along with us?"

asked Sylvie. "I know the queen would love to meet you all."

"We told her about our adventure with you and the polar bear cub," added Trina.

"Wow! A midwinter ball," said Evie.

"It's amazing," said Trina. "It's the best party of the year! We'll have so much fun!"

"Come on," said Sylvie. "We'll take you to a place where Silver can rest and we'll tell you all about it on the way."

"It's not far," added Trina.

The friends chatted as they traveled along the banks of Lake Perla with Odin flying high above.

"Every winter solstice, Queen Aurora has a party to celebrate the longest night of the year," said Sylvie. "You see, we live so far north that in

midwinter it's dark for most of the time. But from tomorrow the nights will start to get shorter and the days longer, and that is something we all celebrate."

"It's a big party with fairies and snow creatures coming from miles around," said Trina. "There will be a feast and lots of music, and Queen Aurora's Fjord ponies will perform their magical dance."

"And you can see the queen's famous display of northern lights in the sky," said Sylvie.

"It's the most amazing display you'll ever see," added Trina. "That's because the snow queen uses enchanted crystals found deep in the mountains. Their magic is so powerful that they fill the sky with dancing colors."

"I can't wait," Evie said, smiling.

It wasn't long before Evie spotted a little wooden shack on the banks of Lake Perla. It was painted white and was almost invisible in the snow, but its windows shone warm and welcoming. Princess Evie knew that

Silver was tired, but the moment that the hut came into view, she could feel her pony's pace quicken.

"Well done," she whispered, resting her hand on Silver's thick coat. "We're almost there."

"We'll take Silver into the hut," said Sylvie. "She can recover from all this snow walking in there."

"It's hard work, isn't it, girl?" said Trina. "But you're very strong."

Inside the shed there was some hay and water ready for Silver to enjoy. The fairies and Evie fussed over the little snow pony, making sure she was comfortable. Evie gave Silver a hug.

"You're safe and snug in here," she said.

"Soon the sun will rise and we will have a couple of hours of daylight," said Sylvie.

"And it will be time for some snow play!" said Trina.

CHAPTER 3

Fun in the Sun

The snow fairies were right—it wasn't long before the sky began to brighten. The sun rose and lit the snow-filled valley with a radiant pink glow.

"Now for some snow fun!" said Trina with a laugh.

"I'm still a bit wobbly on my ice skates," said Evie.

"Don't worry," replied Sylvie. "We're sledding today."

Sylvie and Trina picked up a pair of sleds that were leaning against the hut's wall.

"We've only got these two," said
Trina. "You'll have to share with me,
but that will just make our sled go even
faster."

Silver pulled the sleds up the slope
for them. The food and water had
revived her and she was feeling rested.
Sparkles loved jumping into the
footprints that Evie left in the deep

snow. Odin and the snow fairies flew
with their wings stretched out wide,
warming them in the sunshine. By
the time they all got to the top of the
hill, the sky was clear and blue and
everyone sat down to have a rest.

Evie could feel her cheeks glowing in the fresh air as she looked around the valley. It was breathtaking, with tall pine trees surrounding Lake Perla in snowy clusters and the majestic mountains sparkling in the sun.

"Sunlight is so precious at this time of year," said Sylvie.

"We always try to make the most of it," said Trina.

Sylvie passed around a pouch of dried berries. They tasted deliciously sweet and Evie felt a surge of energy the moment she popped them into her mouth.

"Shall we go down the slope first, Evie?" asked Trina. "You'll have to hold on tight!"

Evie sat behind Trina and before she

knew it, their sled was racing down
toward Lake Perla. It felt as if they
were flying and, although it had taken
a long time to climb up, they were
at the bottom of the hill in seconds.
Trina and Evie landed together in a
heap, looking up at the clear blue sky
and giggling. They were covered in the

powdery snow and Evie was glad of
her gloves and coat.

"We'd better get out of the way!"
said Trina, as Sylvie got ready to whiz
down.

The friends carried on playing in the
winter sunshine until it was time to get
ready for the party.

"Shall we get changed in the hut?"
asked Evie.

"No," said Sylvie with a smile.
"Here."

"But where are our outfits?" asked
Evie.

"Here!" said Trina, laughing and
spinning around in the snow. "All
around us!"

"This is when the fun really starts,"
Sylvie said, taking Evie by the hand.

"We have to make our party dresses," said Trina.

Evie looked around, but couldn't see anything that they could use to make an outfit. All she could see was a mountainside of snow, some trees, and a frozen waterfall.

"All we have to do is draw what we'd like to wear in the snow," said Sylvie.

"Then we decorate our snow dresses with all the beautiful things around us," added Trina. "I'm going to use some of this reindeer moss that I've collected from the trees."

She opened her hand and showed Evie the pale green lichen.

The snow fairies and Evie set to work, helped of course by Odin,

Sparkles, and Silver. While Evie drew
the outline of her dress, Silver scraped
at the snow and found some velvet
moss.

"Thank you, Silver," said Evie as
she collected it with a little help from
Odin. "This is just perfect for my snow
dress's bodice."

Evie found some icicles on the

frozen waterfall in the mountainside
and decided they would make a
beautiful skirt decoration. Sparkles
found some tiny frosty pine cones, and
Evie collected a handful and laid them
out on her snow dress.

"Look, Sparkles," she said. "Those
cones make such a pretty belt."

Silver, Sparkles, Odin, and Evie all
stood back to admire her dress as it lay

glittering in the snow. Sylvie and Trina had finished their party outfits too. Trina had used the pale green lichen to make a fluffy collar and cuffs for her dress of sparkling webs. Sylvie's dress shimmered with frozen leaves and bright berries.

"Now it's time for some snow magic!" said Trina.

She placed her hands on top of Sylvie's. The snow fairies closed their eyes and quietly sang

"Snow falling, frozen sun.
Ice mountains, blue sky fun.
Take the sparkling things we've found,
Icicles, webs, moss from the ground.
Then throw them up into the air,
And give us magical clothes to wear."

They threw their hands up and a flurry of snowflakes exploded from them into the sky. They were all the colors of the rainbow and they danced in the cold air for a few moments. Then they floated to the ground, covering all three snow dresses.

Princess Evie looked up and was stunned to see that the snow fairies were now wearing their beautiful snow dresses. She looked down, eager to see her own dress, but she was still wearing her felt coat.

"Oh dear," she said. "I don't think my dress has worked."

"Let's have a look," said Sylvie.

The fairies led Evie to the frozen waterfall and polished the ice until it shone like glass.

"Take off your coat, Evie," said Trina.

Evie undid the crystal buttons and took off her coat. She gasped when she saw her reflection in the frozen waterfall. She was wearing the party dress that she had made in the snow. The soft velvet bodice sparkled with frost, and the little belt made from Sparkles's pine cones hung prettily around her waist.

"Not bad!" said Sylvie, smiling.

"I love your icicle skirt," said Trina.

Evie twirled and as she did, her icicle skirt tinkled. The friends danced about, admiring one another's snow dresses in the waterfall mirror.

"I think we're ready to go to the party!" said Sylvie.

"I can't wait!" said Trina.

"Come on, Evie," said Sylvie.

But when Evie mounted Silver, she knew right away that something was wrong. Silver neighed and stamped her hoof in the snow. The little Welsh mountain pony's ears had pricked up and her nostrils were flared. She wasn't going anywhere.

"What is it, Silver?" asked Evie.

"I can hear something too," whispered Sylvie.

The friends stood as still as statues and
listened carefully. At first, there wasn't a
sound, but they all heard and then felt a
low rumble that filled the snowy valley.

"Avalanche!" shouted Sylvie.

CHAPTER 4

Moving Mountains

Odin and the snow fairies flew quickly into the air with Sparkles in Trina's arms, but there was nothing Evie and Silver could do except hope that they weren't standing in the avalanche's path. Evie put her arms around Silver's neck.

"Stand fast, little pony," she whispered into Silver's ear. "We'll be all right."

Evie was trying to keep her pony still and calm, but she could feel her own heart racing as she watched the wall of snow come into view. The low rumble

grew to a roar and the sky above them
seem to fill as snow crashed down the
mountainside. Evie could see that the
avalanche was taking everything in its
path—trees and boulders—and she knew
that it wouldn't be long before it got to
where they stood. But as it came toward
them it lost its momentum and grew

smaller. By the time it got to the frozen
waterfall, it had slowed down to a trickle.

"Phew," said Sylvie. "That was lucky."

Everything that had been in the
avalanche's path had disappeared. It
had either been buried or broken. Evie
breathed a huge sigh of relief.

"Stay where you are, Evie," said Trina.
"It takes a few minutes for the snow to set."

"After an avalanche, it takes about
five minutes for the new snow to settle,"
explained Sylvie.

The valley fell silent after the noise of the avalanche. Then, out of the stillness came a voice crying, "Help! Please, somebody. Help!"

The friends looked at one another, amazed, and then the voice called out again.

"Help me!" called the voice. "I'm trapped."

"They sound as if they're deep in the mountain," said Evie.

"You're right," Sylvie agreed.

"We've got to get them out," said
Trina.

"But how could someone get inside
a mountain?" asked Evie.

"Good question," said Sylvie.

"Perhaps they fell down a ravine
trying to escape the avalanche,"
suggested Trina.

"Or maybe they walked behind this
waterfall before it froze over," said
Evie.

"If we can find out how they got in,
then we'll know how to get them out,"
said Trina.

"Let's take a look," said Sylvie. "But
it'll be safer to fly as the snow might
still be unsettled."

Sylvie, Trina, and Odin searched the
mountainside for any crack or crevice
that could let them in. Odin was quite

far when he cawed loudly—he had
found something. The fairies fluttered
up to the spot and Evie could hear
them talking to someone. She couldn't
wait to find out who it was and it
wasn't long before the snow fairies
fluttered down to tell her.

"It's Elva," said Sylvie. "One of
Queen Aurora's snow maidens."

"She was collecting the magic
crystals from the queen's mountain
cave," said Trina, "but she's been

trapped by a huge pile of avalanche
snow. We can't get her out using that
crevice, it's too small."

"We've got to find the entrance
and unblock it," said Sylvie. "Without
the crystals the northern lights can't
happen."

"Elva told us that there's a large
boulder at the mouth of the cave,"
said Trina, scanning the snow-covered
mountainside, "with two silver birch
trees growing beside it."

"Is that it over there?" Evie asked.

She pointed to a large, black boulder that was almost completely covered with snow. It lay halfway up the mountain. "I think you're right, Evie," said Sylvie.

"Come on," said Trina. "Let's take a look; the snow will have set by now."

Everyone rushed over to take a closer look and saw that beside the boulder were two little silver trees almost completely hidden by the

avalanche snow. They began to dig
with their hands, but it was no good—
the snow was too hard.

"It's going to be impossible for us to
move all this snow," said Sylvie.

"It will take us days," agreed Trina.

"Let me see what I've got in
here," said Princess Evie, opening her
backpack of useful things.

As Evie pulled out a pencil and a
pair of scissors, Sparkles found a long
piece of string with a large magnifying
glass tied to it. It landed heavily in the

snow and the sun shone down through the lens, making a bright spark of light to melt the snow beneath it.

"Well done, Sparkles!" said Evie, giving her kitten a hug. "You've found just the thing to soften the snow."

"We'll have to be quick," said Sylvie. "We don't have much time before the sun sets."

Sylvie was right—even though it had been light for only a couple of hours, the sun now hung low in the sky, ready to set. It was getting closer to the mountains by the minute, and very soon it was going to disappear behind them, leaving the northern skies in darkness again.

"We're going to dig you out, Elva!" Sylvie called through the snow.

"You'll be out in no time," said Trina.

The friends looked at one another. They would have to work as a team— and they would have to work fast.

Evie held the magnifying glass high up and aimed the sun's softening rays at the snow. Silver dug with her hooves and Sparkles pushed the melted snow

away with his paws. The snow fairies
and Odin fluttered above, clearing the
snow from the top of the entrance.
They worked as hard as they could,
their shadows getting longer and the
sun getting lower. Evie could feel the
air begin to chill.

"Look," said Trina, pointing.

They turned and watched the golden
sun sink down behind the mountains,
ready for the longest night of the year
to begin.

"What are we going to do now?"
asked Evie. "Even though we've moved
lots of snow, we still haven't gotten
into the mountainside."

The friends stood in the new
darkness, catching their breath and
looking at the huge pile of snow

that they had moved. They were all
exhausted.

"How are we ever going to get Elva
out?" asked Evie.

"What will Queen Aurora say when
she finds out that she hasn't got her
magical crystals for her midwinter
display?" added Sylvie.

"Perhaps we should have gone to her
for help in the first place," said Trina
with a sigh.

Silver walked up to the boulder.
The little Welsh mountain pony dug
her hooves into the snow and leaned
against the boulder. Then she pushed
with all her might.

"Look!" gasped Evie.

Everyone stared in disbelief as the
little snow pony made the boulder

move. It shifted just enough to make
everyone realize what they had to do.

They all dug their feet into the snow,
making sure they had a firm grip, and
then pushed the boulder with Silver.
Because they had melted and loosened
a lot of snow, it wasn't long before they
could feel the rock begin to dislodge.

"It's moving!" cheered Sylvie.

"We're almost there," Trina agreed.

The more they pushed, the easier it was, until suddenly they felt the rock tip.

"Stand clear!" shouted Sylvie.

They jumped back as the boulder rolled away from the mouth of the cave and down the mountainside, racing all the way through the trees to the banks of Lake Perla.

CHAPTER 5

Cave of Delights

A golden light shone from the cave entrance and Evie could see that there was a winding passageway that led deep into the mountain.

"Come on," said Sylvie. "Let's find Elva."

Odin flew in first, followed by everyone else. They went along the passageway that had been cut out of the rock and followed it around a corner. Princess Evie gasped in amazement; she had never seen anything so dazzling.

They were standing in a huge cave
filled with golden light. The walls
glittered with precious jewels and
crystals of every size and color. From
the ceiling hung sparkling gold and
silver stalactites, like giant icicles.

Elva the snow maiden was standing
in the middle of the cave with a
basketful of crystals beside her. Her
white hair shone and shimmered. It
was so long, it almost touched the
floor. The moment she saw her snow
fairy friends she ran up to them and
gave them a big hug. The snow fairies
introduced her to Princess Evie,
Sparkles, and Silver.

"Thank you all so much for coming
to my rescue!" she said.

"We couldn't have done it without

Silver," said Sylvie. "She is the strongest pony in the north."

Elva was amazed when the fairies told her how the little Welsh mountain pony had managed to push the boulder from the cave entrance.

"But how could she?" Elva asked.

"Sparkles found a magnifying glass in Evie's backpack," replied Trina.

"And it melted some of the snow that had fallen in the avalanche," added Evie.

"That loosened the boulder," said Sylvie. "But it was Silver who thought of pushing it out of the way!"

"Queen Aurora will be so impressed," Elva said with a smile, stroking Silver's glittering mane. "We haven't got long before we have to leave for the Midwinter Ball, but as a reward for all your hard work I think you all deserve a little treat. Have a look around and bring me the stones that catch your eye."

Princess Evie looked around. The cave was encrusted with twinkling

crystals of every shape and size. It
was impossible for her to choose any
favorites—they were all so beautiful.
Sparkles, however, had found his
favorite gemstone right away and
was busy playing with a large, round
tiger's-eye crystal.

Evie decided to choose stones in
her favorite colors. She found a pink
rose quartz and a purple amethyst, and
then she spotted a glittering opal that
seemed to have a rainbow inside.

She gave her stones to Elva, who
closed her fingers around the jewels and
gently blew into her hands. When the
snow maiden opened her hands again,
Evie saw a necklace of silver snowflakes.
In the middle of each flake was a
shining rose quartz or an amethyst, but
there was no rainbow opal.

"I thought Silver might like that
one," said Elva with a smile.

Evie looked at Silver and saw the

gleaming opal on her nose band.

"Silver, you look fantastic!" said Evie.

Elva made necklaces for the snow fairies and gave Sparkles a tiger's-eye pendant to hang from his collar.

"Now it's time for us to go," said Elva. "We need to get these magic crystals to Lake Perla."

Evie, Sylvie, and Trina helped the snow maiden with the basket that was filled with the crystals.

"These are heavy," said Evie. "Why don't we put them in one of the sleighs and Silver can pull it? You can ride with Sparkles and me if you want."

"Oh, thank you, Evie," said Elva. "I've always wanted to ride a Welsh mountain pony. The queen has a team of Fjord ponies. You'll meet them when we get to the palace."

Evie and Elva chatted about their ponies as everyone made their way out of the mountain. When they came out of the cave, it seemed even darker than before. The sky was clear and cold and flashing with stars. Evie noticed that the crystals were radiating their rainbow colors and everything around them was lit by their gentle glow.

Evie harnessed one of the sleighs to Silver while Elva loaded the basket of crystals onto it. Trina and Sparkles tied

the basket down so it wouldn't tip or fall on the journey to the snow palace.

"I've never seen jewels like this before," said Evie.

"They are magic and can only be found in this mountain," said Elva.

"Queen Aurora needs them for her display," added Sylvie.

"And she'll be wondering where we are if we don't set off now," Elva said, smiling. "Come on, Silver, let's take the

shortcut. All we need to do is follow Odin."

Odin was waiting for them by the silver birch trees. He turned and shot off down the mountainside toward Lake Perla.

"He knows the quickest routes," Sylvie said. "If we follow him, we'll be at the queen's palace in no time."

Evie, Elva, and Sparkles hopped up onto Silver and away she trotted, with Sylvie and Trina flying above. Off they all went, following Odin into the night.

CHAPTER 6

Snow Wonder

Silver pulled the sleigh steadily through the trees and down into the valley. Evie soon spotted other snow fairies making their way through the night sky to the party.

"Well done, Silver," said Elva. "We'll get there just in time."

Silver took them along the banks of Lake Perla to a flat plain. Standing around the moonlit clearing were lots of snow fairies in their glittering party outfits, fluffy birch mice, a snowy owl, some reindeer, Arctic foxes, and even the polar bear cub that Evie and Silver had rescued the last time they were here. He was standing with his family, but as soon as he saw his old friends he raced over with his mother.

"It's so good to see you again," he said.

"And you," said Evie, jumping down from Silver and giving the cub a hug. "You've grown so much since we last saw you."

"Thank you for bringing the

crystals," said his mom. "Without them we couldn't have the party!"

"This is the moment we've all been waiting for," said the cub.

Evie looked around, but couldn't see a snow palace or the snow queen with her Fjord ponies. The only things in the clearing were some strangely shaped snowdrifts.

"Will you help me, Evie?" asked Elva as she hopped down from Silver's saddle. "We need to put the crystals in the middle of the clearing."

Together, the girls carried the heavy basket into the center of the clearing and placed the crystals in the snow, their glowing colors reflected onto the snowdrifts, making them grow and change shape. Some of the drifts grew into tall snow towers and walls with icicle turrets, others into crystal tables laid with delicious feasts. Evie couldn't believe her eyes as she watched an amazing snow palace grow around them. Soon they were standing in a wonderful ballroom made of ice.

"Wow! You were right!" gasped Evie, astonished. "These crystals really are magic. What a beautiful palace."

Evie looked around at the glittering snow walls and shining crystal floor. The tall arched windows didn't have glass in them and looked out onto the snow mountains. Evie gazed up and saw that there wasn't a ceiling either, just the shimmering stars and moon shining down on everyone.

But most magical of all were the next transformations—the snowdrifts

changing into Queen Aurora with her
six magnificent Fjord ponies.

The caramel-colored ponies had
dark stripes that ran from the tops of
their heads and along their backs to
their tails, making their flowing manes
and tails a mixture of silver and black.
Queen Aurora's hair was the same, and

it was so long that it trailed along the floor. She wore a sparkling white dress and a crown of crystal icicles.

"Welcome to the Midwinter Ball." The queen's clear voice rang out in the night air. "Let the party begin!"

Queen Aurora, Elva, and four other snow maidens mounted their Fjord ponies, who stood proudly in a circle around the crystals that were at the center of the ballroom.

"Silver and Evie," said Queen

Soft music blew into the palace on a gentle breeze. The ponies lifted their heads, whinnied, and then began to perform an intricate dance. Elva was right—Silver knew exactly what to do and joined in with the other ponies, dancing with them in perfect formation. They trotted neatly in diagonal patterns across the ballroom and performed slow canters to make the shape of a snowflake.

"I didn't know you were a dressage pony, Silver," said Evie as her pony performed a three-loop serpentine with Elva's Fjord pony.

Silver tossed her mane proudly while she picked up her hooves in perfect time to the music.

Princess Evie noticed Sparkles was in Trina's arms, watching the ponies

Aurora. "Please come and join us."

Princess Evie was feeling a little confused as she led Silver to the center of the ballroom. How did the queen know her name? What was going to happen next and why did the queen want Evie and Silver to join in? She had no idea what to do. Elva directed her beautiful Fjord pony to stand next to Silver.

"Don't worry, Evie, Silver will know what to do," whispered Elva. "Trust her!"

perform their perfect dressage. He was
spellbound, and so were the rest of the
fairies and animals who stood at the
edges of the room. Evie waved to him
and he winked back at her.

The ponies spiraled around the
crystals faster and faster. The crystals
began to crackle and then their colors
shot up into the starry sky. There was

an explosion of color that filled the sky with curves of light. The energy of the ponies' performance had completed the magic, and now the northern lights were beaming up into the sky from the crystals.

The audience went wild, clapping and cheering. The snow maiden riders, Evie, and Queen Aurora took a bow.

"What an amazing display," said
Evie, looking up in wonder.

"You helped to make it happen,"
said Queen Aurora.

The queen's ponies all whinnied and
whickered in agreement.

"In fact," added Elva, "if it hadn't
been for you, Sparkles, and Silver,
those crystals might still be in the
mountain and the display would not
have happened at all this year!"

"We're so glad we were able to
help," said Evie. "We wouldn't have
missed this for the world!"

"We have been looking forward
to meeting you for such a long time,"
Queen Aurora said, smiling. "Trina and
Sylvie have told us all about you and
your brave snow pony Silver."

"Wasn't she brilliant in the dressage display?" said Elva.

"I didn't even know that Silver could do that," said Evie. "Or that Fjord ponies were so good at dressage."

"Our ponies are very sure-footed and extremely clever," said the queen with a smile. "Never underestimate what your pony is capable of doing. Now, I think it's time for us all to do some dancing and enjoy our midwinter feast."

The northern lights shone down, lighting the ballroom with flashing colors. The dance floor began to fill and soon everyone was having fun swirling and twirling to the beat of the snow fairy band.

Sylvie, Trina, Elva, and Evie danced together in their shimmering outfits

while Silver, Odin, and Sparkles
enjoyed watching the northern lights.

"All this dancing has made me
hungry," Evie said to her snow fairy
friends after some time on the dance
floor.

"Me too," said Sylvie. "Let's see
what there is to eat."

They went over to the tables that
were laden with plates of delicious food.

"I don't know what to eat first,"
said Sylvie. "It all looks so good."

"It does, doesn't it?" agreed Trina.
"I think that I'm going to try a little bit
of everything!"

The friends tucked in and Evie's favorite was the Baked Alaska. The mountain of meringue looked as if it was made of sparkling snow and inside was delicious ice cream with crystal rose and violet flower petals.

"I think I might have to have another helping of that," said Evie. "And then it's probably time for us to go, isn't it, Sparkles? It must be getting late."

Queen Aurora came over as Evie was finishing her second helping of Baked Alaska.

"Thank you for coming," said Aurora. "It has been charming to meet you all."

"Promise us you'll come back," said Sylvie, giving Silver a kiss on the nose.

"Oh yes!" said Trina. "Come back

for our midsummer party! Now, that's
quite a spectacular party too!"

"We'd love to," said Evie. "We've
had so much fun. You were right,
Trina. This has been the most amazing
party ever!"

Evie mounted Silver, and Sparkles
jumped up too, but when Evie asked

Silver to go, she wouldn't move.

"I think Silver wants to say her goodbyes too," said Elva.

"Of course," said Evie. "I'm sorry, Silver. We can't go without saying goodbye to your Fjord friends."

They walked over to the team of Fjord ponies, and Silver said her farewells to them by touching their noses with her own.

"Now it's time to go," said Princess Evie. "I'm beginning to feel quite tired!"

With a pretty neigh, Silver turned and trotted out of the snow castle. Evie was amazed how quickly they found the sparkling tunnel of trees. Before they disappeared into it, she turned Silver around so they could have one last look at the snow palace. The

northern lights shone down from the sky, filling it with colorful lights. Even though they were some distance from the castle, they could still hear music and laughter.

"I think that this midwinter party is going to go on all night!" said Evie, smiling. "But we need to get back and get some sleep. It's been quite an eventful day!"

Silver took them through the tunnel of trees and back to Starlight Stables, where there was still a sprinkling of snow that twinkled in the moonlight.

Princess Evie's ponies were glad to see them back safe and sound, and they whickered and neighed as Evie took off Silver's tack. Evie gave Silver some warm bran mash and checked her over. When she came back from hanging up Silver's saddle and bridle in the tack room, Sparkles trotted up to her, meowing loudly.

"What's the matter, Sparkles?" Evie asked.

The little kitten trotted across the icy stable yard with his tail in the air. He stopped and turned to meow at Evie again.

"All right," said Evie. "I'm coming!"

Evie followed her kitten across the yard and then saw what Sparkles was making all the fuss about. A sled was leaning against the stable wall. Evie took it into the moonlight to have a better look.

"It's beautiful," she said with a gasp.

The wooden sled was painted light blue and it was decorated with hundreds of snowflakes. Just like real

snowflakes, every one was unique!
In the center of each flake was a tiny,
sparkling crystal.

"Thank you, snow fairies," said
Evie. "This is perfect. I can use it to
help me on those icy mornings, and
of course, we can have hours of snow
play, can't we, Sparkles?"

"Meow," agreed Sparkles, chasing a snowflake that had floated down from the sky.

"It looks as if we might be able to use it tomorrow," said Evie. "I think the snow fairies have sent us some more snow."

Evie was right! As she and Sparkles walked up to Starlight Castle, there was a thick white blanket covering the castle grounds . . . and some very strangely shaped snowdrifts!

Pony Facts
&
Activities

Things Princess Evie Likes to Do on a Winter's Day

1. Make a bird cake for the hungry birds at Starlight Stables
2. Eat toasted crumpets
3. Make a hearty bucket of bran mash for all my ponies
4. Snuggle up with Sparkles in front of a warm winter's fire
5. Whiz about on my new sled

Silver

BREED:
Welsh mountain pony

FEATURES:
Hardy and very pretty
with a small head
and big eyes

HEIGHT:
12 hands

COLOR:
All colors except
for piebald and
skewbald

Northern Lights

Evie saw the northern lights with Queen Aurora, Elva, and the other snow maidens. This stunning phenomenon is also called aurora borealis, and it is a beautiful natural light display in the sky.

These sparkly lights are normally seen in the Arctic but can appear lower down in northern countries as well. Similar light displays happen in the Antarctic as well but there they are called the southern lights.

They come in all sorts of different shapes: swirls, curtains, columns, and beams. Some people even say that the northern lights make a noise—like the sound of lots of people applauding.

The northern lights were said to be named
after Aurora, the Roman goddess of the dawn.
People believed the lights looked like her
cloak as she rode through the sky, opening
the gates of heaven for Apollo, the sun god.

Other legends said that the lights were made
when magical foxes made of fire danced and
ran around, making sparks from their tails fly
up into the sky.

Evie's Frozen Treats

Evie loved the special feast they had at the ice palace. Here's a recipe for you to make some frozen treats of your own with the help of an adult.

You will need:

An ice pop mold

Fruit juice of your choice, or yogurt

Fresh fruit, cut up

1. Pour your juice or yogurt into the mold, leaving some space at the top.
2. Add your chopped fruit.
3. Put the mold into the freezer.
4. Remove when frozen and enjoy!

Here Are Some Tasty Combinations to Try!

Summer Ice

Apple juice, strawberries, and raspberries

Totally Tropical

Mango juice, pineapples, and oranges

Strawberry smash

Strawberry yogurt and banana

Choconana

Plain yogurt, honey, cocoa powder, and banana

(mix the yogurt, honey, and cocoa together first)

Berry surprise

Grape juice and raspberries

Fjord Ponies

Queen Aurora and the other snow fairies rode
Fjord ponies in the palace. Queen Aurora
and her snow maidens used the ponies for a
dressage display.

These beautiful horses are originally from
Norway and are one of the oldest breeds of
horses. There are records of them from the time
of the Vikings.

They are very distinctive-looking! One of the things that makes them so recognizable is the dark stripe down their mane. In fact, their manes are often cut to stand straight up and show the dark stripe even more. Sometimes people say they have "zebra manes."

These ponies tend to be quite small but are very strong. Their coat is very thick so they can keep warm in the snowy weather.

True or False

1. Odin is a raven.
2. Evie brought crystals with her to the North Pole.
3. Sparkles is a New Forest pony.
4. The snow fairies make clothes from webs, moss, and icicles.
5. After the avalanche, Evie helped to rescue Elva, one of the snow maidens.
6. Evie met Queen Borealis.

(1.TRUE 2. FALSE 3. FALSE 4. TRUE 5. TRUE 6. FALSE)